THIS WALKER BOOK BELONGS TO:

_____

_____

_____

_____

For Lewis and Mandy

H.H.

First published 1996 by Walker Books Ltd
87 Vauxhall Walk, London SE11 5HJ

This edition published 2003

2 4 6 8 10 9 7 5 3 1

This book has been typeset in Veronan

Printed in Hong Kong

British Library Cataloguing in Publication Data:
a catalogue record for this book is available from the British Library

ISBN 0-7445-9498-7

A Friend for Little Bear

by Harry Horse

WALKER BOOKS
AND SUBSIDIARIES
LONDON • BOSTON • SYDNEY

Little Bear lived all alone on a desert island.

"I wish I had something to play with," he said.

A stick came floating by. Little Bear picked it out of the sea. He drew a picture in the sand.

Then he drew some more.

"I need something else to play with," he said.

He was tired of drawing pictures.

A bottle came floating by.
Little Bear picked it out of the sea.

He filled it up with water,
then poured out
the water
on the sand.

"I need a cup," said Little Bear,
"to pour the water into."

Then something spotted
came floating by. Little Bear
wondered what it was.

"It isn't a cup," he said,
but he pulled it out
of the sea anyway.

It was a wooden horse.

The wooden horse ran round
the island. Little Bear ran after him.

The wooden horse hid. Little Bear
looked for him. They had a lovely time.

They drew pictures in the sand
and filled the bottle again and again.

They played all day long and then
went to sleep under the tall palm tree.

Little Bear woke up.  He rubbed his eyes.

"Look!" he cried. "Lots of things floating in the water!"
He stretched with his stick and pulled out
as many as he could.

"I don't know what these things are," he said,
"but I need them, all the same."

He piled them into a heap.
Then he sighed. "I still
do wish I had a cup."

There wasn't much room
on the island now. Little Bear
had filled it up. He told
the wooden horse
to get out of the way.

"Climb on to that,"
said Little Bear.
"I need more room
for these boxes."

"Look!" cried Little Bear.
"A cup!"

SNAP!

The roof broke.
The wooden horse fell
into the sea and
floated away.

Little Bear was filling his bottle
with water and pouring
the water into his cup.

"Watch me!" he cried.
He filled up the bottle again.
"Watch me!" But no one was there.

He looked up.

He put the bottle down.

He walked all round the island.

"Where are you?" he called.

"I need you!" But no one answered.

"I need my *friend*," said Little Bear.
"I don't need that cup!"

He threw all his things back
into the sea and they floated away.

He sat underneath the
tall palm tree and began to cry.

Little Bear dried his eyes.
Then he rubbed them. Something
spotted was floating by. He ran
and pulled it out of the sea.

"I only need you, Wooden Horse,"
he said, and the two of them
danced for joy on the sand.